BOOK #1

OTTO UNDERCOVER

★ BORN TO DRIVE ★

RHEA PERLMAN

ILLUSTRATED BY
DAN SANTAT

KATHERINE TEGEN BOOKS
An Imprint of HarperCollinsPublishers

This book is dedicated to my loves,
Danny, Lucy, Gracie, and Jake Eboy the First.
And to my fabulous friend Zoe Kurland.

Thanks to these guys . . . Aisha and Chris Marsh and the kids at P.S.
282 in Brooklyn, John (Trippy) Albo, Carol (Feeb) Banever, Amanda
(Cool Beans) Dragon, Jo-el Fields, Maire (It's Grand) Grant, J. A.
(The Best Friend) Kalb, Michael (Burnt Toast) Lessac, Heide (Heed)
Perlman, Steven (Super-Agent) Malk, and Katherine (Master Editor,
Esq.) Tegen.

Otto Undercover #1: Born to Drive
Text copyright © 2006 by Rhea Perlman
Illustrations copyright © 2006 by Dan Santat

www.harperchildrens.com

Library of Congress Cataloging-in-Publication Data
Perlman, Rhea.
    Born to drive / Rhea Perlman ; illustrated by Dan Santat.—1st ed.
       p. cm. — (Otto undercover; #1)
    Summary: After thwarting bad guys to win the Yazoo 200 race, with the help of his trusty
racecar and his eccentric Aunts FiFi and FooFoo, Otto Pillip receives a note from his long-lost
parents inviting him to join the secret family business. Includes words spelled backward,
anagrams, and palindromes.
    ISBN-10: 0-06-075495-8 (pbk. bdg.) — ISBN-13: 978-0-06-075495-2 (pbk. bdg.)
    ISBN-10: 0-06-075496-6 (trade bdg.) — ISBN-13: 978-0-06-075496-9 (trade bdg.)
    [1. Automobile racing—Fiction.   2. Aunts—Fiction.   3. Word games—Fiction.   4. Humorous
stories.]   I. Santat, Dan, ill.   II. Title.   III. Series.
PZ7.P43243Bo 2006   2005006213
[Fic]—dc22   CIP
                                                                                      AC

2 3 4 5 6 7 8 9 10
❖
First Edition

CHAPTER 0

There is none.

CHAPTER REGULAR 1

Otto

His name was Otto Pillip . . .

. . . and he was born to *drive*.

CHAPTER 2

Racecar

What he drove was a racecar. He built it from scratch. It took years of hard work, and sweat, and metal and stuff, too.

His car didn't look like any other car on the track. It had all the speed of a racecar and all the comforts of a luxury sedan, including four doors, a spacious backseat, and cup holders.

He named his car "Racecar." This might seem a little silly. People would probably laugh and snicker like crazy if you named a new baby "Person," but Otto didn't care.

That's because **Racecar** is a *palindrome*. Palindromes are words that are spelled exactly the same backward and forward, and Otto was nuts about them.

He considered himself to be extremely lucky because **Otto** and **Pillip** are both palindromes. He knew that there were plenty of people with one palindrome name, like **Hannah**, or **Bob** or **Brasarb**. But he was pretty sure there weren't many people in the world who had two names that were 100 percent reversible.

An Important Fact

Here's something that Otto doesn't know. Otto Pillip is not his real name. It is a name that was given to him for his own protection.

CHAPTER 3

Not Just Any Old Racecar

Racecar was without a doubt the fastest car on the planet. He had never lost a race. Nobody could beat him, but people still liked to try.

CHAPTER 4

A Race That Wasn't a Race

Otto was at a practice for the Yazoo 200. It was the biggest race he had ever driven in.

The prize was one million dollars. If he won, Otto was going to give the money to the great Dr. Fran Kafmat at Children's Hospital, who was on the verge of a huge discovery. It was some kind of germ blocker that all children would be dipped in at birth, which would put an end to disease as we know it.

There were
only two cars on
the speedway, Car
56 and Racecar.
Racecar's number
was 8, because that
number is the same
right side up and
upside down.

"Watch out on your
right!" came FiFi's
voice over Otto's
headset.

FiFi

Otto had two aunts. He called them The Aunts. FiFi was the smaller aunt. Actually, she was the much smaller aunt. Even Otto was bigger than her, and he was just a

kid. She was always making Otto pick her up and carry her around the house. This was because aside from tap dancing, she hated exercise, even walking from room to room.

What she loved was singing. Too bad she had inherited the family gene for very bad singing. She could only sing one note, A-flat.

She wore a hearing aid because once, when singing a very high A-flat, she blew out her own eardrum.

In spite of her size, she was very strong. She was a master mechanic and could fix any machine ever built. She was co-chief of Otto's pit crew.

Otto called her *IfIf*, which is backward for *FiFi*. This was because . . . sorry, I'll have to tell you later, because this interruption is over.

15

A Race That Wasn't a Race

"What's the matter with that guy? We're not supposed to be racing each other until tomorrow!" shouted Otto, sliding Racecar to the right.

"Maybe he thinks it's tomorrow, because when it was yesterday, today was tomorrow, and he might think it still is," offered FooFoo. "Is it?" she asked.

FooFoo

FooFoo was Otto's
rounder aunt. This
is not surprising,
since food was her
passion. FooFoo
was a brilliant
chef who could
not stop cook-
ing even when
everyone was
full. She also
liked to clean
up. Because she
did everything

fast, she sometimes cleaned up before she served the food. At those times people just had to go out for pizza.

FooFoo could jack up a car and change a set of tires faster than five trained guys. She was the other co-chief of Otto's pit crew. He called her *OofOof*, which is backward for *FooFoo*.

The suspense is over!

ENOUGH WAITING.

The reason Otto called his aunts backward names was because . . .

hold on,

someone's at the door.

Only kidding. The reason Otto called his aunts backward names was because . . . he wanted to.

Next to *palindromes*, Otto was crazy about all backward words. He also loved *anagrams*, which are words that become other words when their letters are scrambled.

He drove his aunts crazy leaving them notes that contained words with mixed-up letters. One time he left a note on the table that said, "I'm in the *eargag*." It took them two days to find him.

Eargag is an anagram for garage.

A Race That Wasn't a Race

Car 56 pulled alongside of Racecar.

"Hey Pillbox, I got a present for ya," said the driver.

"Thanks," said Otto, "but my name is Pillip."

"Sure thing, Pileup," said the driver as he tossed a bag onto Otto's front seat.

Dust exploded all over the interior of Racecar. Otto started to choke. His goggles were covered. Visibility was zero. He had to do something fast. A kid could definitely encounter some life-threatening situations driving at speeds of over 200 miles per hour (mph), especially if his car looked like the inside of the Sahara Desert. Luckily he had just the thing: *voice commands*.

"Forward Adjust," he choked out just as Racecar was going into a spin. The car righted itself on the racecourse. The dust was making Otto gag. He was coughing his head off.

"Sounds like something went down the wrong pipe," said FiFi, who hadn't seen what happened. "Come in and FooFoo will give you the old Heimlich."

"Yes," said FooFoo, "I learned it from old Heimlich himself. He was about 108 at the time. I had to apply it to  him often, because he loved to eat my strudel, but he choked on it on account of he never chewed. It wasn't his fault, though; he didn't have any teeth."

Otto really didn't care. He didn't need the old Heimlich. He needed to see. He felt around under the dashboard and pushed the *Vacu Zap* button. A powerful vacuum started sucking the dust out of the air. In a fraction of a second, it was all gone.

He took a few long pulls of spring water from the straw attached to the watercooler in his racing suit.

He was just starting to feel better

when Car 56 slid alongside Racecar again.

"Hey, Pillpot, I got somethin' else for ya," said the driver. He pulled in front of Racecar. A huge gush of molasses poured out of a chute in the back of his car, onto the tarmac.

Otto had no choice but to squish through it. But the sticky stuff was really slowing Racecar down. He pressed the Tire Wash button on the steering wheel and a strip of brushes and soapy water squirted

out, cleaning the tires in less than a second. Then Otto shifted into high gear and he was off, rounding the track at breathtaking speed. He passed Car 56 with ease.

TIRE WASH

CHAPTER 5

Something Nobody Saw

If someone had stood in Racecar's pit and looked carefully, with powerful binoculars, they would have seen four eyes behind a bush on the other side of the track. If someone had seen these eyes, the troubles of the next day might never have happened.

CHAPTER 6

A Threat and a Large Wallet

Otto brought Racecar into the pit, slowing down from 260 mph to 0 in less than ten seconds, and literally stopping on a dime. FiFi always put one down to make sure.

The Aunts jumped over the rail to take care of Racecar. Car 56 was in the next pit. The driver and his seven huge pit crew guys were sneering at Otto.

"Hey Diplip, I got a news bulletin for ya."

"Yippee," said Otto.

"Tomorrow's news today. Wilson Carlson Fullsom wins the Yazoo 200. Kiddie race car driver cries his eyes out."

The pit crew guys laughed uproariously.

"Good bulletin," said Otto, rolling his eyes.

"And might you be interested in who Wilson Carlson Fullsom is?" asked the driver.

"Oh absolutely, I was just going to ask," replied Otto.

"He's the incredibly good-looking and massively muscled man standing in my shoes!" exploded Fullsom.

You might wonder why Otto didn't say something back to this nasty sack of dirt. But Otto wasn't like that. Aside from the fact that Fullsom was twice as

big as he was, he didn't like spending his energy on dumb stuff. He knew that some guys just couldn't stand the fact that a kid had more brains and imagination in his little finger than they had in their whole bodies. Trying to reason with guys like that was a big fat waste of time.

The Aunts didn't mind wasting their time, however. They dropped their wrenches and jumped right in.

"I've seen better-looking meat loaves," said FiFi.

"Yes," said FooFoo, "I made one last week, and it

was much better looking than you. It was very adorable, actually; I made it in the shape of a bunny."

The crew guys thought this was funny too. They were actually rolling on the ground now.

"Get up!" said Fullsom harshly.

They did.

"Listen to me, pal," said Fullsom. "I bought this here wallet"—he pulled out

what looked like a leather sack. "It's real empty, see, and I need to fill it up. And what I'm gonna fill it up with is the million buckaroos that I'm gonna win in this race tomorrow. So you and your two mommies just stay out of my way, get me?"

FiFi looked like she was about to clobber the lug, which would probably not have ended well for her.

Otto stepped in front of his aunt. He was a pacifist, which is a person who doesn't believe that violence gets you anywhere.

"Thank you for your warning, sir," he said politely. "It's been grand chatting with you. I hope we have a chance to catch up tomorrow. Lovely purse, too."

"Yeah," said Fullsom, who wasn't quite sure what Otto was talking about.

"Come, mommies, let's go home," said Otto, walking to the car.

CHAPTER 7

Mommies?

"We're not your mommies," said FiFi. She was still steaming.

"Certainly not," said FooFoo. "If we were your mommies, then you would be our son, and we would know that, because we would be calling you Sonny Boy instead of Otto, which we most definitely are not."

Otto couldn't help thinking that they

practically were his mommies, and his daddies. They had taken care of him since he was two, when his parents went off on an expedition to discover the eighth continent. Otto didn't remember his parents, but he missed them terribly. He understood why they couldn't be with him, though. Some people have no choice in life but to follow their dreams. He was that kind of person himself.

Otto couldn't ask for better aunts. They had even helped him get a driver's license. This had been very difficult. He had to pass a 30-page written test, which included multiple choice, true-and-false questions, and a 2,000-word essay.

The Aunts understood him completely. They knew that their nephew didn't have time for normal kid stuff. They had written Otto a note to get him out of school for the rest of his life.

CHAPTER 8

The Garage

Otto parked Racecar in the garage, which was his favorite room. It had a loft, which is where he slept, except on the night before a race. This was because Otto had a habit of humming in his sleep, and he didn't want to disturb Racecar. Of course, Otto knew that Racecar was a machine, but he was very close to him anyway, and sometimes even talked to him. This is not so strange when you think that lots of times you will hear grown men talking to their cars and calling them "baby" and "sweet thing."

The garage also had a laboratory for Otto's scientific experiments and inventions. He had been inventing things since he was a baby.

CHAPTER 9

Stuff Otto Invented

1. CRIB ESCAPE ROPE

When he was 8 months old, Otto tore his crib sheets into strips, tied the pieces together to make a rope ladder, hung it off the side of the crib, and climbed down. Staying in a crib just wasn't his thing. Getting out of difficult situations was.

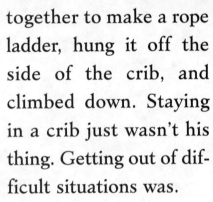

CRIB SHEETS →

← CRIB

← OTTO

2. GYRO SWING-OUT

He was very good at taking things apart, and sometimes he would even put them back together. When he was 11 months old, he took apart the mechanism in his baby swing. He made a few adjustments, and when he was done, the swing went ten times faster and could go in complete circles. He hoped someday to find a cure for the projectile vomiting he experienced every time he went on it.

PROJECTILE VOMITING

3. INDESTRUCTIBLE RUBBER

At 15 months Otto loved chemistry. One day he mixed together his dinner . . . milk, rice, mashed peas, chopped chicken bits, and lime Jell-O. Then he stuffed it into a hollowed-out soccer ball and microwaved it for 21½ hours. The end result was a very bouncy and indestructible rubber. He

glued little pieces of it onto
the paws of the cat,
who to this day can
jump higher than
any other cat and
spends a lot less time
licking her feet.

RUBBER

CAT
GLUE

4. MOTORIZED FURNITURE

HYDRAULIC
SEAT

BRAKE

BABY MOVER

Otto could turn
anything into
a vehicle. He
turned his high
chair into a
baby mover.
By the time
he was three,
he had motor-
ized his aunts'

beds, a supermarket shopping cart, and the living-room couch. Steering was a problem, but with a helmet on, the impact of hitting a wall wasn't really that bad.

5. AUTOMOBILE REMOTE

Probably the coolest thing Otto invented, besides the fastest car in the world, was a fully functional remote control device, with which he could operate Racecar without being in it. The remote was hidden in the inside of a pocket watch that Otto kept on him at all times.

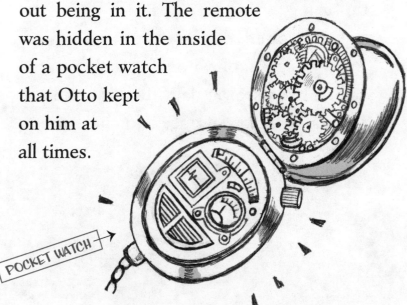

POCKET WATCH

The Night Before the Morning Before the Hour Before the Minute Before the Second Before the Race

"How about some dinner?" Otto said to Racecar. "Just happen to have a fresh batch of the house specialty right here in this can."

Otto opened the can and filled Racecar's gas tank with very finely ground coffee. Espresso, actually. To this he added a touch of Tabasco sauce and chili pepper

oil. Otto had discovered that when mixed with boiling water, this combination was highly combustible, did not pollute the environment, and smelled really good too. He used it instead of gasoline.

"Okeydoke. Now a check of the old vital functions."

Otto went through his checklist: transmission fluid—check, carburetor—check, battery—check, sparks and plugs—check and check, tires—check, all the other stuff—check.

Finally Otto turned the lights in the garage down low, sat in the driver's seat, and sang Racecar a lullaby.

Otto loved to write songs. He was pretty sure that aside from being born to drive, he was born to sing. He had written 73 songs so far. Unfortunately, he too had inherited the family gene for very bad singing. He could only sing in the note of G.

Too Bad I Hid a Boot
(In the note of G)

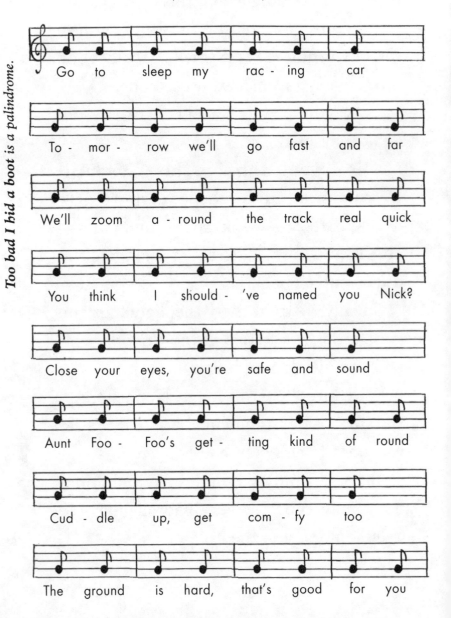

Too bad I hid a boot is a palindrome.

Go to sleep my rac - ing car

To - mor - row we'll go fast and far

We'll zoom a - round the track real quick

You think I should - 've named you Nick?

Close your eyes, you're safe and sound

Aunt Foo - Foo's get - ting kind of round

Cud - dle up, get com - fy too

The ground is hard, that's good for you

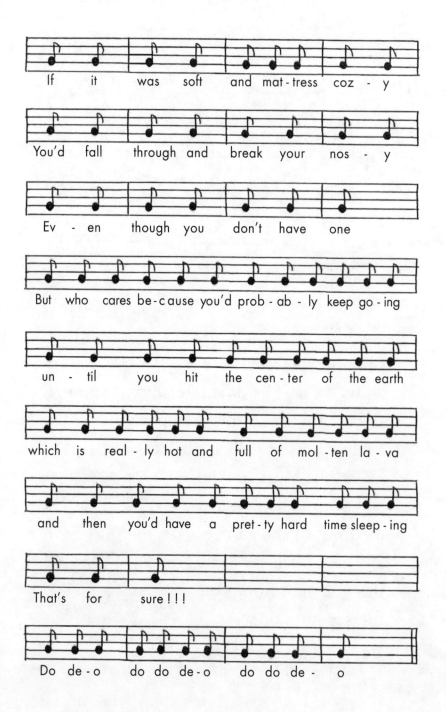

The lyrics to Otto's songs probably wouldn't get him a prize in poetry, but he sure did sing out.

When he was done, he started snoring, since Otto always fell asleep when he sang a lullaby. Eventually his head fell on the horn, and he woke up. Then he tip-  toed out of the garage and went quietly up to the guest bedroom on the second floor.

CHAPTER 11

Uh-oh

That night something *bad* happened.

CHAPTER 12

A Couple of Guys

There were these two bad guys, see, and their names were Ralphie Rhymynchynskn and Paulie Prat. *Prat* backward is *Tarp*. *Rhymynchynskn* backward is *Nksnyhcnymyhr*.

A Couple of Dumb Guys

Now Ralphie was big and fat, and sweat poured off every part of his body even in the winter, so he left a rancid puddle everywhere he stood, and he only had three good teeth and rotten breath like a dragon.

Paulie was skinny and dry. He had extra-bad dandruff, and his skin was always cracking like a shedding snake, and he looked like chalk and smelled like barf.

They were both really mean, and they hated kids and they loved money. They heard about Racecar and how he could never lose a race.

After all, it was in every newspaper, not that they could read. They were both in third grade for eight years, till they got kicked out of school for setting fire to the teacher.

It was Ralphie and Paulie who were behind the bush on the other side of the track, watching Otto practice earlier that day. What they really had their eyes on was that one-million-dollar prize.

"I got an idea how we're gonna win that million-dollar race, Paulie," said Ralphie.

"Ooo," said Paulie, "I had an idea once."

"Big deal," said Ralphie. "Now listen up."

Paulie was excited. "I'm excited," he said.

Ralphie began to lay out his plan.

"Number A: first we're gonna get a junky car that looks a lot like this Pillip punk's car, see."

"Wait, I'll write it down," said Paulie. He got a paper. "Uhm, how do you spell *number*?"

Ralphie ignored him.

"Then we're gonna paint the junk car exactly like his car, see."

"C? I thought you said number A," said Paulie.

"I did say number A, because it's the first number, you idiot," said Ralphie.

"You're the idiot. You're the one that changed the A to a C. What a **boob**," said Paulie.

"Just write, would ya?" said Ralphie. His dripping sweat was starting to bubble.

"Okay," said Paulie, "when you say number A, is that a big A or small a?"

"Who cares?" said Ralphie, trying to stay calm. "Then we're gonna fix up the inside of the car, the seats and the dashboard and whatnot, the same as the kid's car."

"Watnut," said Paulie.

"Get the picture?" asked Ralphie.

"You betcha," said Paulie. "I got it all right here in black and white." He showed Ralphie his notes.

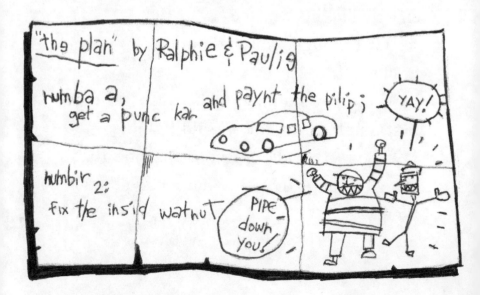

"What a pea brain," yelled Ralphie. "Gimme those." He grabbed the pencil and paper, stuffed them into his mouth, and ate them. "Stop writing and just listen," he said.

"We'll enter the kid's car in the race like it was our car, and we'll win the cash, while the kid is stuck in his garage trying to fix the pile of junk we left him. Get it?"

"Yeah. We win the race and the kid fixes our car. Cool."

Ralphie knocked on Paulie's head. "Hello, is anybody home in there?"

"I don't know, who is it?" asked Paulie.

"Never mind." Ralphie looked down. He was standing in a puddle of sweat up to his shins.

"C'mon, cheese brain," he said to Paulie, "we got work to do."

"Okay," said Paulie, stepping out of a
mound of shed skin flakes, "but I ain't
paying if our car ain't perfect."

CHAPTER 14

Number A

So Ralphie and Paulie found a car, and they painted it just like the picture of Racecar they found in *Cool Cars That Kids Own* magazine.

"We're gonna be rich," said Ralphie, admiring their work. "Let's go!"

They got in the car and floored the gas. The car limped along at 2.5 mph, spewing exhaust and clanging like metal spoons on pots and pans.

"The kid must be a genius if he's gonna fix this," screamed Paulie over the racket.

"He's not gonna fix it, you moron," yelled Ralphie. "We'll never get there this way. C'mon, you gotta push."

Paulie got out of the car. "Aren't you gonna help?" he asked.

"Nah," said Ralphie holding his heart, "bad for my ticker."

"Oh yeah," said Paulie.

He started pushing the car. There was one good thing about Paulie; he was skinny

but he was all muscle. He pushed the car
and ran, too, and when he got bored with
running, he pushed and skipped. Then for
a little variety, he pushed and hopped like
a bunny.

"What a loon," howled Ralphie.

A Horrifying Dream

Meanwhile, Otto was having a very unsettling dream. He was dreaming that a soggy gorilla and a crusty marshmallow took Racecar on a high-speed ride around the world, lost control, and drove him off the end of the earth.

It was 2 A.M.
when they got to
Otto's garage.

Boy, Are They Dumb

"Okay," said Ralphie, "now don't make a sound."

"Right," whispered Paulie, "quiet as a cow."

"Cows ain't quiet," said Ralphie, disgusted.

"I mean one that's not saying moo moo," said Paulie.

Ralphie just stared at him.

"One that's just standing in the grass, swaying."

Ralphie stared harder.

"And it doesn't even have a cowbell on or anything."

To say that Paulie had the brains of oatmeal would be an insult to oatmeal.

"Stop talking," Ralphie whispered loudly.

"You stop talking," Paulie whispered softly.

"You stop talking," whispered Ralphie, even more softly.

"You stop talking," mouthed Paulie soundlessly.

Ralphie grabbed Paulie's lips and pinched them together hard.

Paulie grabbed Ralphie's nose and squeezed it.

Then they head-butted each other. That made them feel much better. They opened the garage.

It took Ralphie and Paulie at least four hours to switch the cars, and it would probably take that long to read how they did it. Reading is a good thing, but four hours is definitely overdoing it, so we'll leave that part out and skip to the next morning.

CHAPTER 17

The Next Morning

Otto got up just after dawn. He ran to wake up The Aunts. He wanted to take them to the pre-race breakfast.

He went into Aunt FiFi's room first. She was a very sound sleeper. Every morning she made Otto put the big part of a tuba over her head and blow it. She

woke up feeling quite refreshed. She claimed it cleared her sinuses, too.

Then he went into Aunt FooFoo's room. She was an even sounder sleeper, so he just brought a bucket of water and dumped it over her head. That was pretty much how she woke up every day. She didn't mind. She said it saved her from having to take a shower.

Otto and The Aunts got dressed and went out to the garage.

They each opened a car door. All three doors fell off. Otto's mouth dropped open. Aunt FiFi gasped. Aunt FooFoo started to cry.

They got into the car. The key was in the ignition.

"Gee, I don't remember leaving it there," said Otto. He turned the key. Nothing happened. He turned it again. Still nothing.

"Third time's a charm," said Aunt FiFi.

Otto turned the key again. The car started to come to life. It was making sounds. Frighteningly, they were less like the sounds of a motor and more like the sounds of a large animal that has eaten too many beans.

Otto released the emergency brake.

It came off in his hand. He put his foot to the gas. The car began to move, sort of. The speedometer read .00001 mph. Otto floored it. It accelerated to .00003 mph.

Fifteen minutes later they reached the end of the driveway.

"I think we're going to miss the always wonderful pre-race breakfast," said Aunt FooFoo. "I'll tell you what. Why don't I go inside, whip us up a nice 'All You Can Eat' buffet, and paper-bag it, nice."

"Oh yes," said Aunt FiFi, "I'm starving. Turn off the car, Ottie, we have to wait for your aunt."

"That's all right," said FooFoo. "*Breakfast* will only take me 20 minutes; I'll meet you at the next mailbox. I'm a *fast baker*."

"Will you two cut it out!" said Otto. "Racecar is having a total breakdown."

Fast baker is an anagram for breakfast.

64

Otto got out of the car and opened the
hood. He almost had a heart attack.

"This isn't Racecar. This is an impostor!"

"Are you sure?" asked both aunts.

CHAPTER 18

Otto Answers

"Yes,"

answered Otto.

CHAPTER 19

The Miserable Paperboy

"I'll prove it to you with my remote."

Otto took out his pocket watch and opened it up. The tiny remote was hidden under the clock, which flipped up when he pressed a button.

Otto spoke into the remote.

"*Go,*" he said. Nothing happened.

"*Reverse,*" he said. Nothing.

He gave every command he could think of. Racecar did not respond.

"Okay, everyone, stay calm," shouted Aunt FiFi, who turned into a general in difficult situations. She marched around the garage, barking out orders.

"Let's try to figure out what's happened here. Everyone take a deep breath!" she ordered.

"Yes, breathing is good," said Aunt FooFoo.

Otto didn't feel like breathing, even though it was usually one of his favorite things to do.

"Don't you get it?" cried Otto. "Someone stole Racecar!"

"I don't think he breathed," said FooFoo.

"Definitely not," said FiFi.

Just then the miserable paperboy came by on his bike and threw the newspaper into the driveway. It hit Otto on the head. Otto knew he did it on purpose.

He grabbed the paper and was about to throw it back when he glanced at an ad on the front page. It said:

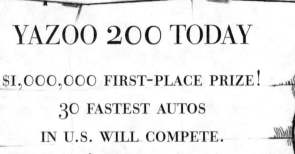

YAZOO 200 TODAY

$1,000,000 FIRST-PLACE PRIZE!

30 FASTEST AUTOS

IN U.S. WILL COMPETE.

Toto, DON'T JUST STAND THERE

READING . . .

GET TO THE *crate rack*!

TICKETS AVAILABLE AT THE BOX OFFICE.

That's a very unusual ad, thought Otto.

"I wonder who *Toto* is, and what's a *crate rack*?" he said out loud.

"Well," said FiFi, "Toto is the little dog in *The Wizard of Oz*."

"Yes," said FooFoo, "and a crate rack is the place in his doggie box where Dorothy hangs his leash."

"I don't think so," said Otto, in deep thought.

Otto had heard that when someone gets

70

an idea, it's like a lightbulb going off in their head. In his case, it worked the other way around.

"Hit me with the lightbulb," said Otto.

FiFi climbed a ladder and held a 100-watt bulb over his head.

"I've got it," cried Otto. "Why didn't I see it before? *Crate rack* is an anagram for *racetrack*. And *Toto* is me!"

"Ahh, the stress is too much for him,"

Toto is an anagram for Otto.

said FooFoo to her sister. "He thinks he's a puppy."

"No," said Otto. "Don't you get it? That ad contains a hidden message telling me to get to the racetrack! C'mon, let's go."

"Carry me," said FiFi.

Otto picked her up and they raced out of the garage.

CHAPTER 20

They're Off!

He carried her and ran the whole five miles to the racetrack.

Otto practically flew through the starting gate, but it was too late. The green flag went up and the cars were off. He was just in time to see Racecar, with the ugliest paint job in the history of automobiles, take off in the lead.

Otto ran up to the racetrack administrators.

"Stop that car!!!" he yelled. "Call off

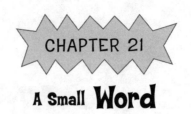

CHAPTER 21

A Small Word

the

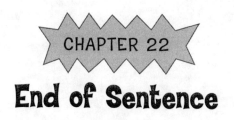

CHAPTER 22

End of Sentence

race."

CHAPTER 23

Paulie in the Pit

Yo banana boy is a palindrome.

No one could hear him above the roar of the engines. Otto ran to the pit. There was Paulie, sitting on a lawn chair, dunking a banana into a giant tub of soda, shedding skin all over everything.

Otto was really stressed out, but he couldn't pass up a good palindrome.

"Yo banana boy," he shouted, "what do you think you're doing? Who's in my car, and why is there snow all over my pit box?"

Paulie stomped on Otto's foot and swatted him away.

"I don't know what you're talking about," he said. "Don't start pushing me around, pip-squeak. I hate kids. I'll knock your block off. I don't know what car you're talking about, and this is Otto's pit, not yours."

"I'm Otto," said Otto.

"Oh," said Paulie, "why didn't you say so? Did you fix our car yet? Where is it? We ain't paying if it ain't perfect."

Otto had the feeling he was talking to someone whose brain was out of order.

Just then Racecar came roaring around the track. Stinky Ralph sweat was seeping out through the doors and windows. The car was weaving all over the road.

The other drivers were doing their best to avoid being hit. They were all yelling things like, "Get off the track, creepo." "You couldn't drive a tricycle with training wheels." "Where'd ya get your license, Kmart?"

Wilson Carlson Fullsom in Car 56 was overjoyed. He couldn't believe his luck. Without Otto driving Car 8, he had no doubt that he was going to win the race.

The starter was waving the black flag at Racecar, which means "Get off the track,"

but Ralphie didn't know that, and he didn't care.

"Do you know that guy?" asked Otto.

"Sure," said Paulie, "he's my best friend, except he's really like my brother, except we don't have the same mother, and we don't have the same father, and we don't have the same house, and we don't have the same clothes, and we don't have the same arms, and we don't have the same face—"

Otto interrupted. "Well, you see how he's driving all over the road? That's because he needs an adjustment on his craveshnasengrudergreeger. He'll never win the race that way. Wave him into the pit, and I'll fix it for him."

Craveshnasengrudergreeger is not a backward word. It's not a word at all. Otto was just trying to get Ralphie to bring his car back.

"Oh yeah, I knew that, toad face," said Paulie. "I was just picking up my arm for waving."

The next time Ralphie came around, Paulie waved. Ralphie waved back.

Paulie waved some more.

"Come on in, your cravenmainer is broken," he shouted.

Ralphie started to steer Racecar toward the pit, but at the last minute he saw Otto standing there. He turned Racecar around sharply, skidding in the mud, narrowly missing two other cars coming down the straightaway at 210 mph. Otto had to think quickly. It was tough without a lightbulb.

CHAPTER 24

¹/₄ of a Second Later

He was still thinking.

$^1/_8$ of a Second After That

Some more thinking.

1/16 of a Second After That

It was coming to him.

Record-Quick Thinking

The remote control!

Otto pulled out his pocket watch.

"You know what, you pile of reptile peels," he said to Paulie, "I'm gonna give your buddy a ride he'll never forget."

"Oh good," said Paulie, missing the point. "He'll like that."

Otto spoke into the remote, *"Manual Override, Remote Mode!"*

Otto was now driving the car, even though he was standing in the pit.

"Spin Out!" he said.

Racecar did a 360-degree turn, then another half turn, and ended up facing in the wrong direction with all the other cars coming toward him.

Ralphie screamed and grabbed the

wheel, frantically trying to turn the car around. Nothing happened.

Otto said, *"Forward,"* and Racecar took off.

Otto was maneuvering him the wrong way on the track, dodging to the left, dodging to the right, expertly missing the other vehicles.

Then Otto spun Racecar back around, zigzagged him over to the track infield, and brought him to a complete stop.

Paulie was clapping his hands and whistling through his teeth.

"Hey, pretty good driving there, for a car with a broken creamingravy," he yelled to Ralphie.

Ralphie was sweating more than he ever had in his whole life, and shaking like a leaf in a tidal wave. He tried to get out of the car.

"Maybe later," said Otto, and he quickly pressed the button for the child-proof lock. Otto whispered into the remote, and Racecar took off like a rocket.

Ralphie was flung to the other side of the car. Otto said, *"Rear Wheel, Rise."*

Racecar rose up on his front wheels. It was like a handstand. Ralphie's face was pushed up against the windshield.

Then Racecar came down on his rear wheels, bucking like a wild bull. Ralphie was yelping like a prairie dog with a toothache.

CHAPTER 28

Lunch

That's when The Aunts showed up. FooFoo was wheeling FiFi in a shopping cart. She had made a quick stop at the market across the street. After all, no one had eaten any breakfast.

FooFoo piled up Muenster cheese, cottage cheese, salami, shrimp, peanut butter, tuna fish, onions, coleslaw, mustard,

mayo, A.1. steak
sauce, hot pepper,
and maple syrup into
a giant sandwich.

"Eat!" she
demanded of Otto.

Otto took a bite
even though he
wasn't hungry,
because he knew
that arguing with his aunt about food was
useless. She had been known to force-
feed people before.

Paulie was drooling.

"Gimme that," he said, grabbing the
sandwich.

"Who are you?" asked FiFi.

"I'm the car thief," said Paulie proudly.
"That's my partner out there doing tricks
in this kid's car."

FooFoo grabbed the sandwich back

and started pelting Paulie with the pine-apples she had bought for dessert.

"Ooo, pineapples are my favorite kind of apples," he said.

He caught one of them in his hands and tore off the spikey skin with his teeth. Then he stuffed the skin in his mouth and threw away the juicy yellow part.

CHAPTER 29

That's It for Those Guys

Otto was having a pretty good time with the remote. He tried some moves he had learned from watching ice-skaters.

Paulie was getting angry.

"Stop fooling around," he yelled to his partner. "Why don't you just drive the car around in circles like the other drivers? Did you forget about the prize *m-u-n-e-e*?"

Paulie pulled a stop sign out of his Everything You Need to Be a Bad Guy Kit

TRIPLE TOE LOOP

and walked across the track to Racecar.

This threw the race into complete pandemonium as racecars skidded to screeching halts, trying to avoid hitting him. He left a line of white flakes across the ground as he passed. Some drivers thought that this was a new finish line.

"All right, big shot, move over. Paulie's driving," he said to Ralphie.

Before Paulie could get into the car, Otto gave the remote another command.

A large shovel shot out of the front of Racecar and *Scooped* Paulie up. Then Racecar rocketed backward toward the pit. The g-force pushed Ralphie's ears and cheeks up past his nose. The scooper dumped a dazed Paulie at Aunt FiFi's feet.

"Ride's done," said Otto, and spoke one more time into the remote.

The roof of the car opened, and Ralphie was ejected. He was propelled 120 feet straight up and then started down, raining sweat all the way. Many people in the stands put up their umbrellas.

Only Paulie held out his arms. "I got you, big guy," he yelled.

Unfortunately for Ralphie, his trusty partner was turned the wrong way. Ralphie crashed to the ground directly behind Paulie and then went right through the cement and kept on going, boring a hole deep deep deep into the earth.

CHAPTER 30

They're Really Off

The race was stopped. None of the drivers knew what to do. The officials made a ruling.

"The Yazoo 200 will continue with Otto Pillip driving his own car. Wilson Carlson Fullsom in the lead car has completed 31 of the 200 laps in 22 minutes. Racecar is in last place, having finished only 3¼ laps. All drivers prepare for the flag."

Otto put on his helmet. Fullsom, in the next pit, put on his helmet. He caught Otto's eye and growled.

"Ooo, scary," said Otto.

Now Otto had to close his mind to everything but the road in front of him. Concentration. Concentration. Because he was a superstitious guy, there were certain things he had to do before every race.

First he kissed his right hand and touched the roof of the car. He did this four times.

Then he knocked on his helmet twice. Then he opened and closed his hands around the steering wheel eight times.

The flag went up.

He whispered, *"Race fast safe car."*

The flag came down. They were off.

Race fast safe car is a palindrome.

said over the headset.

"Got you covered," said FiFi.

FooFoo was watching the other side of the track.

FiFi said, "56 on the inside of curve four."

Otto responded, "Going to the outside."

But Fullsom's pit chief had hacked into Otto's headset frequency. He could hear everything they were saying, and repeated it to his boss.

"The kid's going outside," he said.

Fullsom moved to the outside.

CHAPTER 31

More Trouble

Racecar was around the track before the other cars had even begun. Still, they were going to need more than a fast start to have a shot at winning this race. He was going to have to go where no car had ever gone before. Into *Hyper-Supreme Speed*. Otto switched gears.

Racecar was speeding around on the tarmac like a moving bullet. It looked like the other cars were standing still. They kept out of his way.

But Fullsom was fearless. He was going to run Otto off the road.

Otto figured that Fullsom would try to get in his way.

"*OofOof*, *IfIf*, keep your eyes on 56," he

FiFi yelled, "Slide left, now!!"

Otto put on the brake and went left, narrowly missing Car 56.

Seconds later, coming around the next lap, FooFoo yelled, "56 on the left of straightaway, after curve three."

Otto responded, "Okay, I'm going right."

Fullsom's pit chief yelled, "Move right."

"Watch your right side," said FiFi. "He's in front of you."

This time the cars actually scraped against each other, but Otto pushed the *Right Wheel Rise* function. Racecar skidded by on his left wheels only.

Then Otto figured it out. These guys had to be monitoring his transmissions.

He knew exactly what to do. Just for fun, he had programmed Racecar to be able to respond to backward commands. He had no idea it was going to come in this handy.

"Edoc, Edoc!" he shouted.

FooFoo and FiFi got the message.

Fullsom's pit chief got the message too, but he didn't understand it.

"Edoc, Edoc," he yelled.

"What are you talking about?" asked Fullsom.

"Edoc?" he said meekly, not having a clue what he meant.

"What should I do?" asked Fullsom angrily.

FooFoo said, *"Evruc owt, yats edisni."*

The pit chief of Car 56 said, *"Evruc owt, yats edisni."*

Fullsom said, "Stop speaking Russian."

"Tog ti," said Otto.

"Tog ti," said the pit chief.

"You're fired," said Fullsom as Otto zoomed past in the inside lane.

Edoc, edoc is backward for Code, code.
Evruc owt, yats edisni is backward for Curve two, stay inside.
Tog ti is backward for Got it.

CHAPTER 32

And the Winner Is . . .

Now Otto was cruising. He felt fine. Great, actually. To Otto, driving fast was the most natural and relaxing thing in the world. The faster he went, the more relaxed he felt.

"Slow down, acci—" came over his headset, too late.

FooFoo didn't have a chance to finish her sentence, and Otto didn't have a chance to slow down. It was terror on the tarmac!

The massive accident happened right in front of him. Five cars crashed into one another, two of them spinning out of control. Being an outstanding driver, he didn't hit any of the cars, but there was oil and metal all over the track.

Something struck Racecar's front axle.

It cracked, and the wheels spun wildly, bolts flying everywhere. Otto had no choice but to return to the pit.

He had 5 laps left to go in the race. Fullsom had 12, but he had avoided the accident completely.

FooFoo and FiFi jumped over the pit wall. Otto decelerated way too quickly. His heart felt like it was leaping out of his chest.

"Oxygen!" shouted FiFi. FooFoo brought him the canister.

"Give it to Racecar," gasped Otto.

Fullsom was catching up. He had four more laps under his belt. Eight to go.

It took 38 seconds for FiFi to weld the axle together. Then she pushed the tire ejection switch and the tires flew off.

"Move, move!" she yelled to her sister.

FooFoo slapped on the new tires with a speed previously unknown in tire-slapping history. She even had half a second left to get the sandwich and stick it into Otto's

mouth as he jumped into Racecar and took off again.

Otto spit out the sandwich. It took eight seconds to get Racecar up to full speed. Otto did three laps and found himself right next to Fullsom. They both had one lap left. All Otto had to do was pull out in front, and he would win.

"You're not goin' anywhere without me, Snotto," Fullsom yelled.

A hook shot out of Car 56 and grabbed on to Racecar's open window. The two

cars were now attached.
Racecar was pulling Car
56 along. They were coming
up on the last curve and
straightaway.

"Thanks for the ride, Blotto," shouted
Fullsom, who was planning to release Otto
right before the finish line and shoot
across it for the win.

Otto smashed his hand onto a button
on the steering wheel, activating his
Swindow, which was a window with a
saw on top. The saw quickly made metal
filings out of the hook.

"Sorry I can't stick around, Fullofit,"

said Otto, "but there's a million dollars over there with my name on it." Otto sped forward.

He crossed the finish line 2¼ tire lengths ahead of Fullsom.

CHAPTER 33

Good Times, Good Times

Otto drove Racecar into Winners Way for the presentation of the first-place prize.

Everyone at the race was in a party mood. Everyone except Wilson Carlson Fullsom. He was in his pit, bawling like a baby. Otto almost felt sorry for him. He thought of bringing him a tissue.

Nah.

The Chief Executive Governor of Automobiles was there to do the presentation.

"Otto Pillip—ahem ahem." The Chief was always clearing his throat. "For your superb driving—ahem—and coming in first in the Yazoo 200—ahem ach ach—I would like to present you with—ahem ach ach ahem—this really big prize."

"Thank you," said Otto, putting out his hand to take it.

"Well, actually, it's not so big, because it's a check—ahem achchch achach—and checks are kind of small compared to a great big trophy or an elephant or something—ahem ahem ahem, ahem, ahem," said the Chief, holding on to it.

"It's just perfect," said Otto, trying again to take the check.

"This isn't right," said the Chief to his assistants. "Otto's just a little tyke. Ach ach ach ach. What's he going to do with an

itty-bitty piece of paper? Don't we—ach ahem ach—have something great for the kid, like a train set or a kite or something— ahemaaaccchh?" The Chief was really out of it when it came to gifts for kids.

"That's all right, sir, I really like the piece of paper," said Otto firmly. He took the check out of the Chief's hand.

"Here you go, Dr. Kafmat," he said, handing over the check.

"Otto, congratulations on winning the race, and thank you very much. I feel like *now I won*. I am going to name my earth-shattering germ blocker, The Pillip, in your honor," she said gratefully.

"Hey, Dr. Kafmat, did you know that *now I won* is a palindrome?" asked Otto.

"Yes, and be careful with those. They can be habit forming. I've often had to treat children with severe cases of palin-dromitis."

"What do you give them?" asked Otto worriedly.

"**Lonely Tylenol**, of course," said the doctor, cracking up.

Then she left for the lab, because she had no time to waste when the well-being of children was at stake.

Otto was doing the twist. He always did the twist when he was happy.

"Let's celebrate," he said.

"Yes, I'll cook," said Aunt FooFoo. "Liver and onions for everyone!"

A lot of people gagged.

"Just joking," said FooFoo. "I'll make a nice parmesan-coated eel with an anchovy walnut sauce, and a nice linguini with snails."

"Huh?" said everyone.

"Just joking some more," said FooFoo. "I'll make pasta with sauce and some garlic bread, nice."

"Yes," said FiFi, "and I'll entertain!"

"Uh huh," said FooFoo. "Free earplugs for everyone!"

CHAPTER 34

Ralphie and Paulie

Back at the pit, a geyser had erupted. Scientists said it was caused by a big man with overactive sweat glands being jammed into a deep, narrow hole in the earth.

The rescuers couldn't get to Ralphie, but Paulie thought he could fish him out, even though the biggest fish he had ever caught was a shoe. So they built a prison around him and gave him a fishing pole. They dropped a snorkel down to Ralphie.

Ralphie wasn't just swimming around, either. He had found a sharp rock embedded in the walls of the earth. All day long he chipped away at the bottom of his prison.

Every once in a while, Paulie would check on his progress. "How's it goin', my good man?" he'd yell down the hole.

"Goin' great!" Ralphie would holler up in a gurgly voice. "In a year or two, you're gonna still be up there playing with your fishin' pole, and I'm gonna be lying on the beach, sipping pink drinks, on one of those tropical islands like South America."

"Suit yourself," yelled Paulie. "But I ain't goin' anywhere 'til the kid gives us our car back."

CHAPTER 35

Otto Finds
Something Out

The party at The Aunts' house went on into the night, with everyone eating and singing and doing the twist.

FiFi chose an aria from the great opera *The Barber of Seville* by Rossini, where Figaro, the barber, tells everybody what a great guy he is.

She sang, "Ahh bravo Figaro! Bravo, bravissimo, bravo, lalalalalalalala. Figaro, Figaro, Fi-ga-roooo."

Boy, could that make your head hurt!

Otto left the party early. He wanted to give Racecar a fresh paint job right away.

It was quite late when he finished. Otto was cleaning up his paintbrushes when The Aunts came in.

"Otto, your aunt has something to tell you," said FooFoo.

"Yes, I do," said FiFi. "I'm the Barber of Seville, Figaro, Figaro, Figarooo—," she started singing.

"Not that!" said FooFoo. "The paper . . . give him the paper."

"Right," said FiFi.

In a secret compartment in her hearing aid was a teeny folded paper. She gave it to Otto.

"After the race, a man with a coat over his face gave this to me. He said it was a note from your parents. I put it in my ear for safekeeping."

Otto's heart started beating fast. He had never gotten any kind of letter from his parents before.

He unfolded the paper, which took forever because it had about 200 folds.

Finally, when it was all opened, he sat down to read it. But the paper was blank. There was nothing on it. His heart sank. And he was angry, too. It was a rotten trick to play on a kid.

"Wait a minute," said FooFoo. "I know what this is," and she took the paper out of his hands.

She put it on a plate and poured cold water over it. This made Otto even more upset.

"You don't have to destroy it," he said. "It's just a piece of paper, but it's the only thing my parents ever gave me."

His aunt paid no attention to him. She then took four tablespoons of hot water and mixed it with four teaspoons of ammonia. She filled a dropper with the mixture and started dribbling it over the plate.

Otto thought she had lost her marbles. But suddenly something miraculous happened. Red letters started to appear on the paper. Otto jumped back so hard, he landed on the motorized platform on the fire pole to his loft and shot up to his bedroom. He quickly slid back down the pole.

"Invisible ink," he sputtered. He could hardly get his breath.

"They made it with *phenolphthalein*. That's one of my favorite chemicals because backward it's *nielahthplonehp*."

He carefully lifted the paper out of the water and spread it out on a table. It said:

Eee YiiiY Eee • Super Agents

Dearest Dear Jake, our son, who thinks his name is Otto but it isn't,

It is time for you to know the truth. Your real name is Jake Eboy. Our real names are Eleanor and Hogarth Eboy. We are not really looking for the eighth continent. Who needs another continent? We are secret agents working for *Eee YiiiY Eee*. We have been chosen to defend the earth against lousy people, and that's what we have been doing these many years. We need you,

Eee YiiiY Eee is a palindrome.

son, and we hope you will join the agency.

You have a great talent, our boy. Any function you want Racecar to have, you can invent, and we know you'll be coming up with some doozies. Remember, nothing is out of reach. If you can imagine it, you can make it happen.

If you accept, you will receive your assignments in code, and work undercover. No one must ever suspect you are an Eboy. We have plenty of enemies who wouldn't mind hurting you just because you are our son.

If you accept, The Aunts will disguise themselves and accompany you on your missions, because the minimum age for solo secret agenting

is 18. You don't need a disguise, because you are a fast grower, and in a few weeks people who have known you all your life will say, "You can't be Otto . . . you've gotten so big, I don't even recognize you." Also, it is a fact that most adults and all bad guys have a genetic defect that prevents them from telling one kid from another.

If you accept, go into the bathroom, dump the contents of the shampoo bottle down the drain, and at exactly **10:01** P.M. flick the lights on and off three times. (Actually the shampoo has nothing to do with it, but we know how much you hate to wash your hair.)

Then keep an *eye* out for your next assignment.

10:01 is a palindrome.   Eye is a palindrome.

eye

Eee YiiiY Eee • Super Agents

Jake, we want you to understand that secret agenting is a very dangerous business. We are 100 percent proud of you already, and we always will be, even if you decide you would rather be a florist.

We love you very, very much. For instance, infinity is pretty big, and we love you way more than that.

Always remember, *Jake* backward is *Ekaj*. Eboy backward is *Yobe*.

Love,

Mom and **Dad**

P.S. Burn this letter immediately. It would be a disaster if it fell into the wrong hands.

Mom and Dad are both palindromes.

Otto ran to the bathroom, dumped the shampoo down the drain, and at precisely **10:01** P.M. he flicked the lights three times.

He said good night to The Aunts and he read the letter one more time. Then took out a match and lit it. The problem was, he didn't seem to be able to bring his hand to the paper. He knew he should burn the letter like his parents told him to, but it was too important to him.

What he did was this. First he memorized every word. Then he reversed the chemicals and made the writing invisible again.

Then he folded the letter hundreds of times until it was just a teeny speck and hid it in a second secret compartment behind the main secret compartment in his remote control pocket watch.

CHAPTER 36

Jake, But We'll Still Call Him Otto

Otto didn't remember ever being this happy before in his whole life.

He lay down on top of Racecar's hood and looked up at the stars he had painted on the ceiling.

"I'm pretty sure my parents had something to do with that message in the newspaper, don't you think?" he asked Racecar.

"Definitely," Otto answered himself.

"I have a feeling that I'm going to have to be really good at figuring out mixed-up words if I'm going to be a great secret agent," he continued.

"Yup, that's for sure," Otto replied to his own comment.

"I wonder how we're going to find out what our next mission is," he said.

Before he could answer himself, he had a panicky thought.

"They told me to keep an *eye* out. I hope they're not confusing me with Mr. Hoffenkagen down the street, who has a glass *eye*, and is always taking it out and showing it to everyone."

"Nah, I don't think so either," Otto said, relieved.

He started drifting off.

"Did you know that **mom** and **dad** are both palindromes?" he asked.

"So is *tuna nut*," he said truthfully as he slipped off to sleep, humming happily in the note of G.